Copyright © 1999 by Nord-Süd Verlag AG, Gossau Zürich, Switzerland
First published in Switzerland under the title *Albin und Lila*
English translation copyright © 1999 by North-South Books Inc.

First published in the United States, Great Britain, Canada,
Australia, and New Zealand in 1999 by North-South Books,
an imprint of Nord-Süd Verlag AG, Gossau Zürich, Switzerland.
First paperback edition published in 2002 by North-South Books.
Distributed in the United States by North-South Books Inc., New York.

A CIP catalogue record for this book is available from The British Library.
Library of Congress Cataloging-in-Publication Data

Schami, Rafik, 1946–
[*Albin und Lila*. English]
Albert & Lila / by Rafik Schami; illustrated by Els Cools and Oliver Streich; translated by Anthea Bell.
p. cm.
Summary: Albert, the only white pig on the farm, and Lila, a chicken too old to lay eggs,
suffer the ridicule of their fellow animals until they join forces and defeat a hungry fox who comes to call.
[1. Pigs-Fiction. 2. Chickens-Fiction. 3. Foxes-Fiction. 4. Individuality-Fiction.]
I. Cools, Els, ill. II. Streich, Oliver, ill. III. Bell, Anthea. IV. Title. V. Title: *Albert and Lila*.
PZ7.S3337A1 1999 [E]-dc21 99-18980

ISBN 0-7358-1182-2 (trade edition)
1 3 5 7 9 HC 10 8 6 4 2
ISBN 0-7358-1183-0 (library edition)
1 3 5 7 9 LE 10 8 6 4 2
ISBN 0-7358-1693-X (paperback edition)
1 3 5 7 9 PB 10 8 6 4 2
Printed in Germany

For more information about our books,
and the authors and artists who create them,
visit our web site: www.northsouth.com

Rafik Schami
Albert
& Lila

Illustrated by Els Cools
and Oliver Streich

Translated by Anthea Bell

North-South Books
New York · London

ONCE UPON A TIME there was an old farmer who kept a great many pigs and chickens. They were very happy in the farmyard. There was always enough to eat and drink, the rooster had a lovely dung heap where he perched every morning, crowing to welcome the sunrise, and the pigs had a big muddy puddle to wallow in after dinner.

The chickens and the pigs were very polite to each other, and when they met they would say, "Good morning!" or, "Good evening!" or, "How do you do?" And they always called, "Sleep well!" before settling down for the night.

But the chickens never played with the pigs.

"Pigs can't even fly over the fence," said the chickens. They couldn't understand why the pigs liked rolling on the ground and wallowing in the mud.

The pigs never played with the chickens, either.

"Chickens are silly. They can't do anything but lay eggs and fly," grunted the pigs, turning up their noses at the chickens.

The chickens were content with their life, and if it hadn't been for the fox, who sometimes crept through the broken window into the henhouse and carried off a hen, they would have been the happiest chickens in the world.

Of course, the pigs weren't afraid of the fox, so all of them were perfectly happy.

All of them?

No. Albert was not a happy pig. Albert had been born with white skin, not pink skin like the rest of the pigs, and the others all laughed at him. When they played hide-and-seek, Albert was always the first to be found, however hard he tried to hide.

Just once it took quite a long time before anyone found him. That was in winter, when there was snow everywhere. Albert stood very still, smiling happily to himself and pretending to be a stone statue. But then snowflakes started falling. They tickled his nose. Albert couldn't help it—he sneezed.

The other pigs started laughing, but it wasn't kind laughter. "That silly old statue sneezed! That silly old statue sneezed!" they chanted, and they didn't want to play with Albert.

So Albert spent a lot of time on his own, dreaming of a world where all the pigs were white.

One day Albert saw an old chicken scurrying out of the henhouse, clucking in alarm. The rooster had chased her away in a rage, and the other chickens were cackling at her. "You nasty old hen!" they clucked. "You thief! Lay your own eggs!"

The terrified chicken was breathless by the time she reached the far corner of the farmyard, where Albert was sitting.

"What happened?" asked Albert kindly.

The old chicken took a deep breath and shook her head. "Oh, it doesn't matter. You see, I'm old and I can't lay eggs anymore. If the farmer finds out, he'll put me in the cooking pot. There are forty of us hens, so I asked the others if they would lend me an egg every now and then. That way, the farmer would never notice."

"Why not? Can't he count?"

"The farmer doesn't count the eggs," explained the chicken, "but if he sees I never have any in my nest, he won't even give me water to drink, and then . . ." Here she began to weep bitterly.

"Dear me!" cried Albert, horrified.

"I told the others I would repay them by telling their chicks stories when they were too busy," sobbed the chicken, "but they wouldn't even listen! The rooster chased me away. Nobody likes me!"

"Well, *I* like you," said Albert, "even if you don't lay eggs. What's your name?"

"Lila," said the chicken. "Do you really and truly like me?"

"Yes indeed! Come on, let's play together!" said Albert.

"Look at that, will you? Albert's gone crazy. He's playing with a chicken!" said the pigs, shaking their heads.

"What did I tell you?" crowed the rooster. "Lila's gone crazy. Maybe it's not surprising, at her age! Just look at her dirty feathers. That's what happens when a chicken starts playing with a pig."

Of course the hens joined in the rooster's mockery, but that didn't worry Albert and Lila. They kept inventing new games, and they never stopped laughing all day long.

When it was evening, the two of them decided to stay out in the yard. They hid in the hay until the old farmer had closed the doors of the pigsty and the henhouse, and they heard his heavy footsteps as he went home.

There was a full moon that night. Albert and Lila sat on the dung heap and looked at the moon, the stars, and the fields all around. They told each other their dreams, and never noticed how fast the time was passing.

When day dawned, they hid deep in the hay again. Soon the farmer came to open up the pigsty and the henhouse, and the rooster crowed, but Albert and Lila stayed snoring in their hiding place until noon. And as the days passed, they became dear friends.

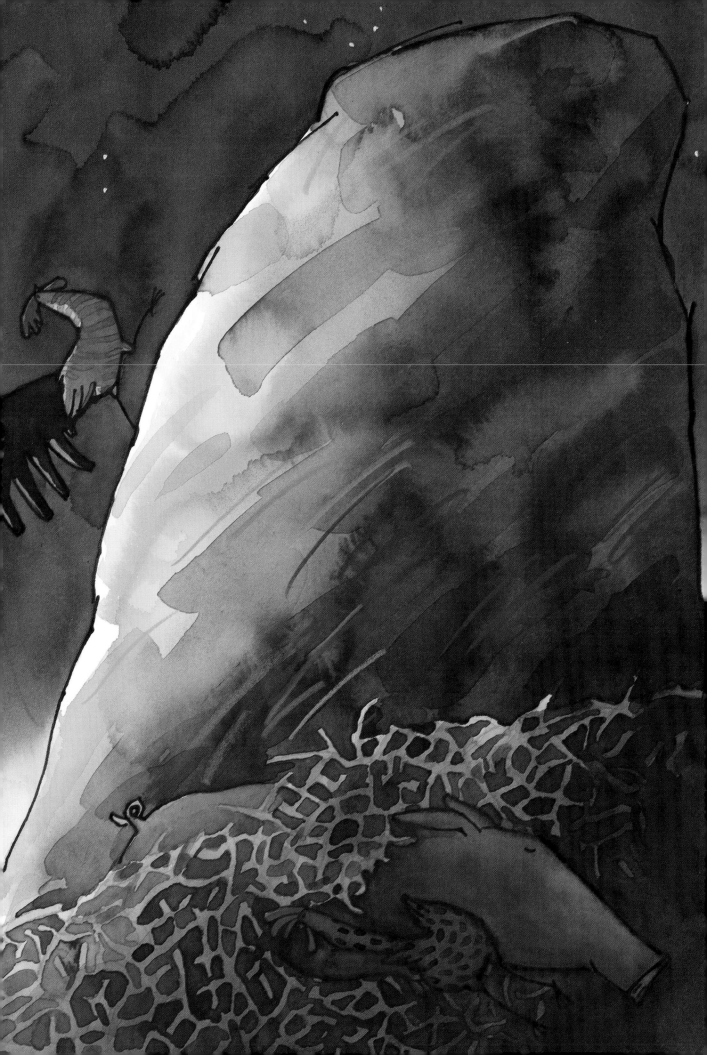

One night they were both gazing
into space again, lost in thought.
    The full moon was casting its beautiful
silvery light over the fields once more.
Albert and Lila never tired of looking at
the wonderful landscape. But suddenly
Lila gave a start of alarm. She stretched
her neck to get a better look—sure
enough, there was the fox!
    "It's the fo . . . the fo . . . the fox!"
stammered Lila.
    "Don't be scared of the fox! I'm here
to protect you," said Albert proudly.
    "Yes, but what about the others?"
whispered Lila. All her feathers were
standing on end.
    Albert thought for a moment. Then
he said, "Come on, I have an idea." He
told Lila his plan. Chuckling quietly,
the two of them hurried over to the
henhouse.

Lila climbed up on Albert's back and undid the bolt of the door. While Albert slipped cautiously into the henhouse, Lila ran back to the pigsty, fluttered quietly through the open window, and hid under the sill. None of the pigs noticed anything, but over in the henhouse the rooster woke up when Albert tripped over a feeding bowl on his way to the window.

"Now that crazy hen is bringing the pig home with her!" said the rooster crossly, and the chickens all clucked too.

"Shh! Keep quiet! The fox is outside!" whispered Albert.

"Oh dear, oh dear, the fo . . . the fox!" cackled the chickens in alarm.

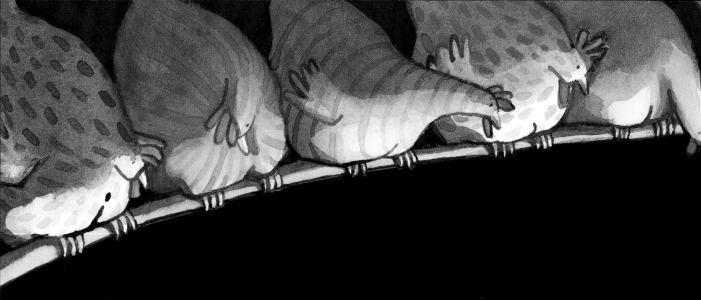

By now the fox had reached the henhouse, and he was about to creep in through the broken window as usual. What a shock he had when he saw Albert on the other side of it!

"Well, old fox, and how are you tonight?" Albert asked the surprised fox.

"Oh . . . oh, fine, thanks, but . . . er . . . what are you doing here? This is the henhouse, you know!"

"Oh no, we pigs are living here now. The chickens have been moved to what used to be the pigsty," said Albert, raising his voice.

Over in the pigsty, Lila began clucking quietly.

"Thanks for the tip!" said the fox, relieved to hear that telltale clucking. "I didn't know pigs were helpful to foxes. When I tell my friends, they'll never believe me."

"Oh, don't mention it," said Albert. "But watch out—those chickens have put on a lot of weight recently."

"Glad to hear it. I'm ravenous!" said the fox, his mouth watering.

The fox turned, ran across the farmyard, and took a great leap into the dark pigsty.

The pigs squealed in alarm, ran frantically around the sty, and knocked the fox over. Every time he tried to get up again, another huge pig kicked him to the ground. The terrified fox yelled with pain, and shouted for help so loud that it made the chickens laugh. For the first time ever, they weren't afraid of the fox.

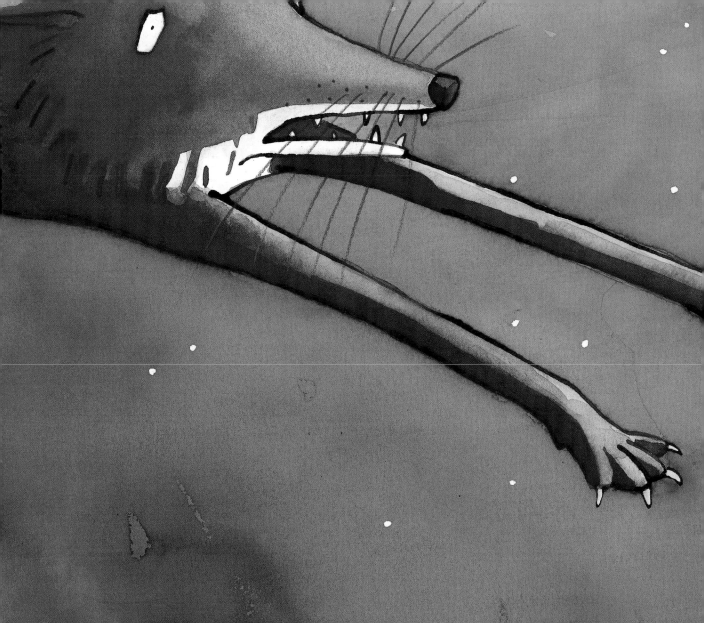

"This farm must be bewitched!" groaned the fox. "The chickens have changed into pigs!"

With great difficulty, he squeezed through the pigsty window and out into the open, and then he ran for his life, swearing never to set foot in the farmyard again.

"I told you those chickens had put on weight!" Albert shouted after him. The sound of Albert's laughter rang in the fox's ears as he made his escape.

The rooster thanked Albert and Lila. He felt ashamed of being nasty to Lila just because she couldn't lay any more eggs. And the pigs were proud of Albert, who had tricked the wily fox. They all wanted to play with him now.

But Albert still liked playing with Lila best.